Silly Goofy

BY

Sylvie H.B.Y.

ILLUSTRATED BY

Agnes C. & Silver L.

Published by **KOALAFUL** , a U.S. based company

www.koalaful.com

ISBN: 978-1-942509-99-8
Printed in PRC.

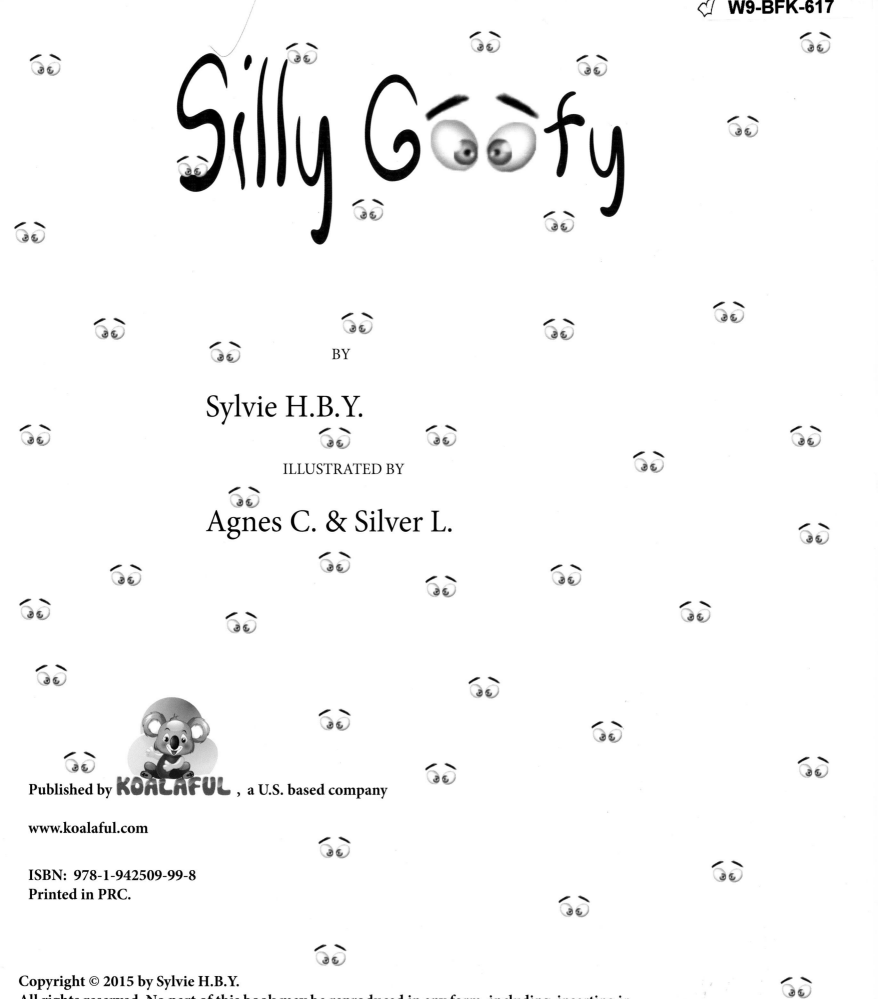

...pon a time there was a boy who was
...ut wasn't. His name was Goofy—or
... his last name was Goofy—and his first
...was Silly.

...oofy came from a long line of
... Williams. Silly Goofy's father was
... William the 137th, Silly Goofy's
...father was William William the 136th,
...s great-grandfather was William
...n the 135th.

All the way back to his great great-grandfather, Peter Williams the forgetful, who lived in London hundreds of years ago and was—you guessed it!—terribly forgetful. So he gave his son two names exactly the same so he could remember them.

Having two exact names was working out fine until five years ago, when William William the 137th, Silly Goofy's father, was registering his son's birth at the town courthouse. Well, the smallest events can change history and—wouldn't you know it?—William William the 137th had hiccups that day.

So when the court registrar was taking down the name, William William the 137th let out an enormous hiccup. Instead of saying "William William," he said, "SsssSilly Goofy," which is what it sounds like when you hiccup and say "William."

Could he have changed the name?
Well, of course, but William William the 137th was a man of
his word who didn't like to correct himself.
Also, it would have cost five bucks and William William the
137th didn't like to spend money if he didn't have to.
"What's the worst that can happen?" he said to himself.
And being very unimaginative, his answer was,
"Not much."

Sadly for Silly Goofy, a lot can happen with a name like his. Poor Silly Goofy was very confused throughout his childhood. His mom would tell him,
"Your name is Silly Goofy." But then if he started to make mischief, Silly Goofy's mom (who was called Jane Jane the 112th, as imaginative names didn't run on either side of the family) would say,
"Don't be silly, Silly" or "Don't be a Silly Goofy, Silly Goofy."

Many years later, a very expensive doctor with a very big title would tell Silly Goofy that he had existential angst. But all Silly Goofy knew was he got very, very confused and he didn't really know who he was.

With a name like Silly Goofy, Silly Goofy grew up to be a very, very serious and quiet child. If people always think you're going to be silly, then you learn to be very, very sensible.

So Silly Goofy could always be found with his hair neatly combed, his clothes tucked in and his nose stuck in a book. This made life even tougher for Silly Goofy because his mom and dad sort of expected him to be silly. I mean, if it says "beans" on a can, you would expect it to contain beans, wouldn't you? And if it says "silly" on a kid, you would expect him to be silly, wouldn't you?

Things got worse for Silly Goofy back when he was 3 or 4 and started school. And school, as everyone knows, is no place to be silly. Not unless you expect to spend a lot of time outside the principal's office. With a name like Silly, Silly Goofy was in trouble from the first day of school when his teacher, Mrs. Jennifer Orange, was laying down the 'no silliness' rules with her class.

ABCDEF
GHIJK
LMNOP
QRSTU
VWXYZ

"Do we have any silly billies in this class?" she demanded.
"Yes, Mrs. Orange!"
called Silly Goofy.
"Are you being silly?"
inquired Mrs. Orange.
"I'm always silly,"
answered Silly Goofy.
"And how long do you plan on being silly may I ask?"
asked Mrs. Orange.
"Until I save up five bucks to change my name,"
said Silly Goofy. And that is what caused Silly Goofy to spend
his first day at school sitting outside the principal's office.

Silly Goofy learned a tough lesson that day: sometimes when you've done nothing wrong, you still get into trouble.

That whole first year was a tough, tough year for young Silly Goofy. At every morning assembly, the principal asked all the children to promise that they wouldn't be silly that day.

Silly Goofy couldn't join any of the sports teams because the coach said it was dangerous to be silly on the field.

Silly Goofy even had a girl that he had his eye on. Sybil Jennison had red hair, freckles, and probably had no interest in the silliest boy in school, especially when all the other children made fun of him.

Unlike when other children at school were teased for being clumsy or ginger or both, no one could say the children were being rude to Silly Goofy; they were just calling him by his name.

And that probably would have been how the story would have gone, all the way until Silly Goofy was the silliest boy to graduate from college. Except that fate took a funny turn one day.

Carluccio's Amazing Circus came to town one day. And just as Silly Goofy was a silly boy who wasn't, Carluccio's Amazing Circus really wasn't all that amazing.

Its clown was sad; its acrobats had broken legs; and the locks on the cages for its animals were rusty. Now most of the time that didn't matter, because the only animals Carluccio's had were cats. Old man Carluccio would paint stripes on them and pretend they were tigers.

But one day, Mr. Carluccio bought a real tiger named Jeffrey from an old zoo. And tigers and cages with rusty locks are a terrible combination. Jeffrey escaped and headed to Silly Goofy's school.

The principal announced over the intercom,
"There is an escaped tiger in the school cafeteria. The police
and the Army have been called."
All the children ran away in terror, except for Silly Goofy
who sat and listened.
"Only a silly person would approach a tiger. Being close to a
giant, man-eating tiger is a very silly thing to do," the
principal continued.

Mrs. Orange kept the children in her classroom while they were waiting for the police, the Army, and whoever else you call when wild tigers are loose.

"Where are Sybil Jennison and Silly Goofy?" Mrs. Orange demanded. The class told her that Sybil had been in the cafeteria collecting recycling (she was a most considerate girl). No one knew where Silly Goofy was.

Just as Mrs. Orange was
thinking about how one
would explain to a parent
that their child had just been
eaten by a tiger, something
remarkable happened...

out of the school walked Jeffrey the tiger, with Silly Goofy riding upon his back and Sybil sitting behind him with her arms wrapped around him!

Jeffrey had been so used to people running away from him and screaming, that when a silly boy approached him and said hello, Jeffrey hadn't known what to do.

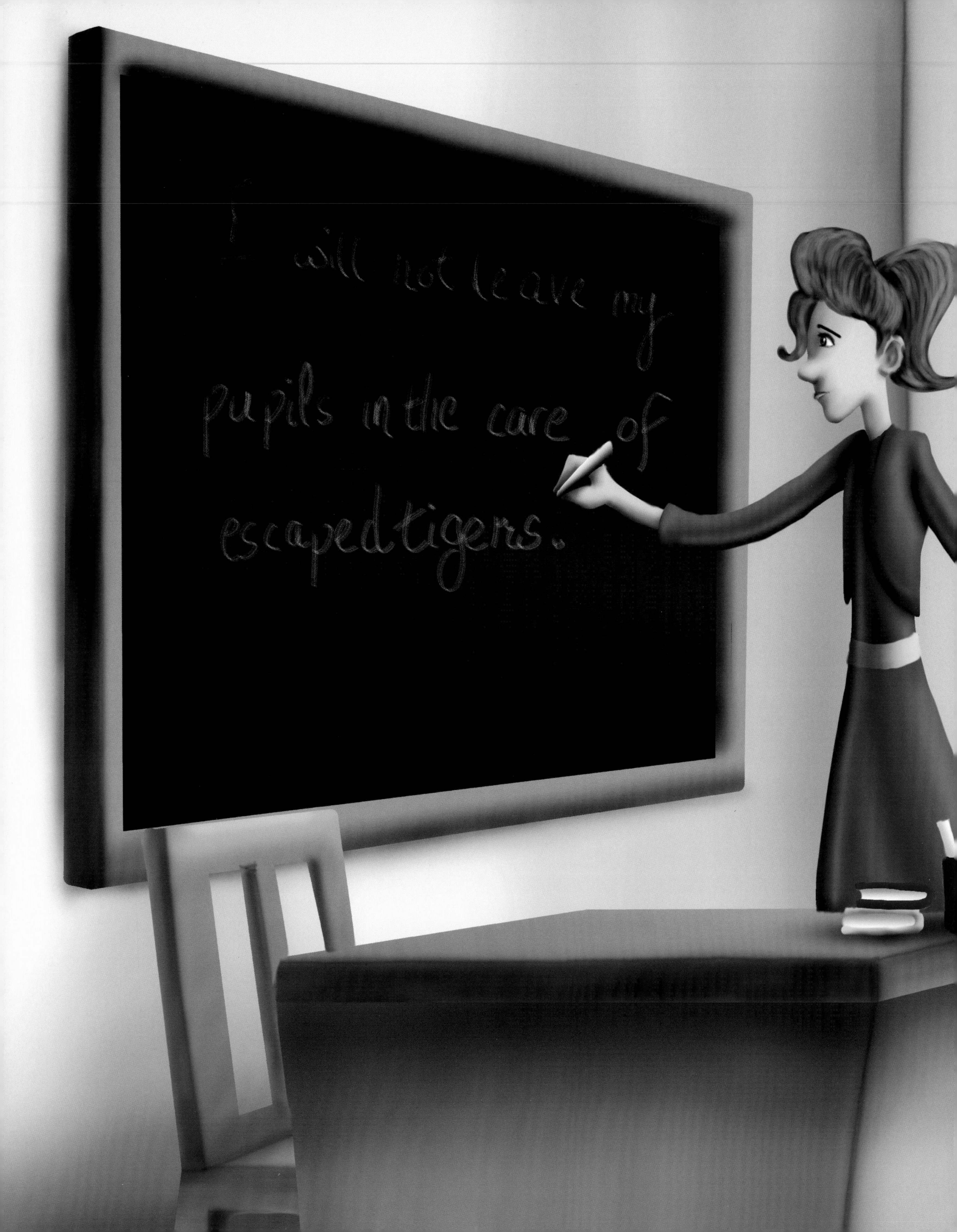
I will not leave my
pupils in the care of
escaped tigers.

Jeffrey had been more than happy to be led outside.
And here our story ends.
Jeffrey was allowed to live in a home for retired zoo animals.
Mrs. Orange had to write a 1000 times on the blackboard,
"I will not leave my pupils in the care of escaped tigers."

As for Silly Goofy, he was given a five-dollar reward for capturing an escaped tiger. But Silly Goofy didn't spend it on changing his name; he had realized that names aren't that important after all.